EEK & ACK

THE BLACK HOLE REPORT

written by
BLAKE A. HOENA

illustrations by
STEVE HARPSTER

Raintree is an imprint of Capstone Global Library Limited, a company incorporated in England and Wales having its registered office at 7 Pilgrim Street, London, EC4V 6LB – Registered company number: 6695582

www.raintreepublishers.co.uk
myorders@raintreepublishers.co.uk

ISBN 978 1 406 27567 4
17 16 15 14 13
10 9 8 7 6 5 4 3 2 1

British Library Cataloguing in Publication Data
A full catalogue record for this book is available from the British Library.

Printed in China by Nordica.
1013/CA21301916

TABLE OF CONTENTS

Chapter 1

Ack liked school. Galaxy exploration class was his favourite subject.

Today in class, he would get to learn about a strange, new place.

"Students, I am going to hand out your research homework," Mrs Grym said.

Ack could barely sit still. He was so excited.

"I will give each of you a space object to explore," Mrs Grym said.

"That will be fun," Ack thought.
"Maybe I'll get to visit a planet
where people speak in armpit noises.
I can already toot the alphabet up
to P!"

"After you are done, you will write a 100-page report on what you learned," Mrs Grym added. "Now everyone, collect your subjects."

The students rushed to the front of the class.

Mrs Grym handed Ack a piece of paper with two words on it.

"Black hole!" Ack shouted. "But I don't know anything about black holes."

"That's why it's called research," Mrs Grym said.

BBRRRIIINNGGG!

The final bell rang. Class was over.

The other students jumped up and raced for the door.

Ack walked slowly to his bus.

Chapter 2

EEK HELPS ACK

Ack slumped down in the seat behind his brother, Eek.

"What's wrong?" Eek asked.

"I have to write a report on black holes," Ack said. "I don't know a thing about black holes."

Eek grabbed Ack's sheet of paper.

A big grin spread across his face.

"That gives me an idea!" he said.

"Oh, no," Ack said. His stomach

started to hurt. "Your ideas always

scare me."

"Do you want help with your homework or not?" Eek asked.

"Um . . . I guess so," Ack said.

Ack wasn't sure if he trusted his brother. But he did need help.

As they got off the bus, Eek told Ack his plan. "You need to see a black hole with your own eyes. And I know just where we can find one," he said.

Chapter 3

THE Z UNIVERSE

Eek and Ack raced to their spaceship. They climbed in, blasted off, and zoomed away from planet Gloop.

"So why are you really helping me?" Ack asked. "I don't believe you are just being nice."

"I wanted to test my new whizzler drive," Eek said. "Hold on!"

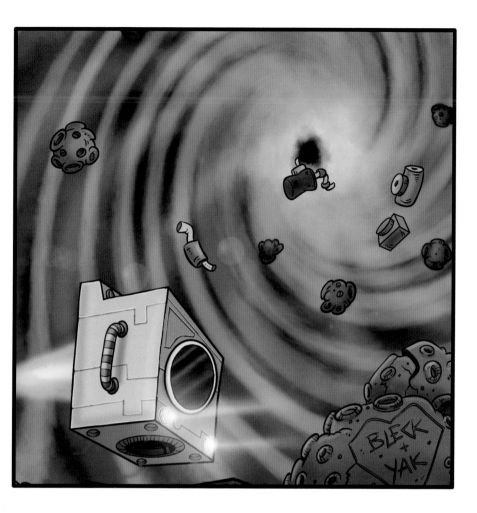

Their spaceship zipped across the
galaxy. Soon, they reached the black
hole. Rocks and space junk swirled
around them.

"Let's get closer," Ack said.

"Ack, stop!" Eek shouted. "Don't you know anything about black holes?"

"No, that's why I'm doing research," Ack said.

"Black holes are like giant vacuum cleaners," Eek said.

But it was too late. They flew too close. The black hole sucked up their spaceship and threw it around.

"Aaaahhhh!" Eek and Ack screamed.

When their spaceship shot out
of the other side of the black hole,
another spaceship appeared.

Two pink and fuzzy creatures were
inside the spaceship. Their voices
echoed through a speaker.

"Welcome to the Z universe," one of them said.

"We're Zeek and Zack," the other creature said.

Then together they yelled, "Do you need a hug?"

The pink creatures grinned out at Eek and Ack's spaceship.

Two big furry arms reached out
and hugged Eek and Ack's spaceship.

"Eek!" Ack screamed.

"Ack!" Eek cried.

"They are pink and fuzzy!" they
shouted together. "And they're
hugging us!"

"Fire the shove-a-tron!" Eek shouted to Ack.

Slam! The shove-a-tron pushed Zeek and Zack's spaceship away.

"Wait! Come back. Let's hug some more," Zeek and Zack said happily.

"Ah!" Eek and Ack cried in horror.

Eek spun their spaceship around.

He headed back into the black hole.

"Let's get out of here!" yelled Eek.

"But I didn't get to do any research," Ack said. "I'm going to get a Z on my report!"

"Hey, that's the same mark I got on mine," Eek said.

"Oh, no!" Ack said. "It's even worse than I thought!"

ABOUT THE AUTHOR

Blake Hoena has written more than 20 books for children. He once spent a whole weekend just watching his favourite science-fiction films. Those films made him wonder if he could invent some aliens who had death rays, hyperdrives, and clever equipment, but still couldn't conquer Earth. That's when he created the two young aliens Eek and Ack, who play at conquering Earth just like earthling children play at beating villains.

ABOUT THE ARTIST

Steve Harpster has loved to draw funny cartoons, mean monsters, and goofy gadgets ever since he first starting using a pencil. At school, he preferred drawing pictures for stories rather than writing them. Steve now draws funny pictures for books as his job, and that's really what he's best at. Steve lives in Ohio in America and has a sheepdog called Doodle.

GLOSSARY

black hole an area in space that sucks in everything around it

exploration the act of studying something or somewhere unknown

explore to travel in order to discover what a place is like

galaxy a large group of stars and planets

horror great fear or shock

research to collect information about something

shove-a-tron a long arm-like machine on Eek and Ack's spaceship that is used to push away dangerous things

slumped sank down heavily

swirled moved around in circles

whizzler drive a machine on planet Gloop that makes alien spaceships go very fast

TALK ABOUT THE STORY

1. Ack did not like his research topic. Have you ever been given homework from school that you didn't like at first? Was it as bad as you expected?

2. Which object in space would you like to explore? Why?

3. Eek offers to help Ack in the story. Do you help your brothers, sisters, or friends? Do they help you?

WRITING TIME

1. Carry out your own research about black holes and write a paragraph about what you've learned.

2. Pretend you are in a galaxy exploration class, and you get to travel to outer space. Write a story about what you see.

3. Compare Eek and Ack to Zeek and Zack. Make a list of similarities and differences.

EXPLORING THE UNIVERSE
with Eek & Ack

It's no surprise that Ack was worried about his research topic. Black holes are difficult to study.

These places in space have very, very strong gravity. Gravity is a force that pulls things in. Anything that comes too close to a black hole will be pulled in and disappear, even light.

A black hole is formed from a dying star. As a star's gases burn, heat pushes out from the star into space. Then the star's gravity pulls the heat back in.

But when a star gets older, it runs out of gases. The heat stops pushing out from the star, but gravity keeps pulling in. The star gets smaller and smaller, until it seems to disappear. What's left is a black hole.

The scientists who study black holes have a hard job. Black holes are billions of miles away. They are also invisible. If scientists tried to send up special machines to get a closer look at the black holes, the gravity would damage the machines.

So scientists have to study the area surrounding the black hole. They use special telescopes to see what happens to things around the black hole.